DATE DUE

JUN 28 1989	MAR 23 1992	OCT 06 2003 JAN 02 2014
AUG 22 1989	JUN 02 1992	OCT 24 1995
AUG 28 1989		
	JUN 25 1992	SEP 21 1998
OCT 21 1989		OCT 19 1995
JAN 20 1990	FEB 23 1993	
FEB 22 1990	MAY 4 1993	APR 26 2000
MAR 21 1990	SEP 13 1993	JUN 25 2002
APR 25 1990	OCT 20 1993	JUN 09 2004
JUN 20 1990	JAN 12 1994	DEC 18 2010
NOV 29 1990	MAY 23 1994	
JAN 22 1991	JUN 22 1994	DEC 07 2011
	MAY 24 1995	DEC 28 2011
MAR 14 1991		OCT 31 2012
MAR 25 1991	JUL -5 1995	
NOV 21 1991		MAY 30 2013
FEB 24 1992		

The Storekeeper

The Storekeeper

Tracey Campbell Pearson

Dial Books for Young Readers | New York

Published by Dial Books for Young Readers
A Division of NAL Penguin Inc.
2 Park Avenue
New York, New York 10016

Published simultaneously in Canada
by Fitzhenry & Whiteside Limited, Toronto
Printed in Hong Kong by South China Printing Co.
(a)
First Edition
1 3 5 7 9 10 8 6 4 2

Library of Congress Cataloging in Publication Data
Pearson, Tracey Campbell.
The storekeeper / by Tracey Campbell Pearson.
p.   cm.
Summary: Follows the activities of a storekeeper
from early morning when she opens her shop
until it is time to go home.
ISBN 0-8037-0370-8. ISBN 0-8037-0371-6 (lib. bdg.)
[1. Stores, Retail—Fiction.] I. Title.
PZ7.P323318St 1988   [E]—dc 19   87-36602   CIP   AC

The art for each picture consists of an
ink, watercolor, and gouache painting that is
color-separated and reproduced in full color.

For the Dessos

Early, early every morning
while the rest of the town is still asleep

the storekeeper

starts her day.

It's time to open the store.

Good morning to the doughnut man,

to the road crew,

and to the sleepy children on their way to school.

All the town stops in

to say good morning!

The storekeeper has a busy day.

She must tidy her store

and sort the mail

while her customers look around.

Mrs. Bond buys a lot. Miss Dickerson, a little.

Hank from the road crew stops by to say hello.

Salespeople bring her fancy things from far away

and special things from right next door.

The storekeeper buys what she thinks

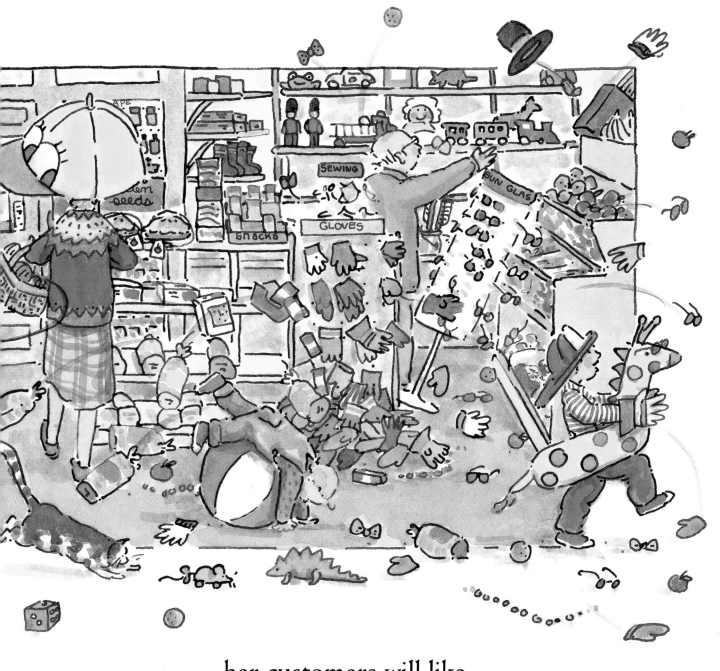

her customers will like.

Evening finally arrives.

Still her customers come and go

until late at night,

when her work is done,

and the storekeeper says

to all the town

good night!